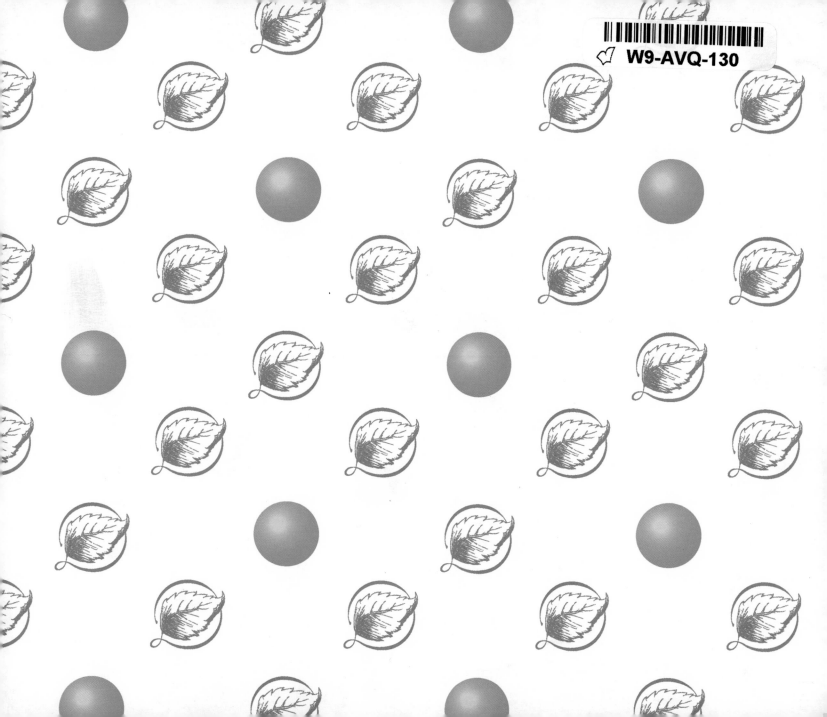

Mr. Sanchez and The Kick Ball Champ

Written by
Laura Appleton-Smith

Illustrated by
Keinyo White

Laura Appleton-Smith was born and raised in Vermont and holds a degree in English from Middlebury College. Laura is a primary schoolteacher who has combined her talents in creative writing and her experience in early childhood education to create *Books to Remember*. Laura lives in New Hampshire with her husband Terry.

Keinyo White is a graduate of the Rhode Island School of Design with a B.F.A. in illustration. He currently produces children's books and freelance illustrations from his studio in Los Angeles. This is his third book from Flyleaf Publishing.

A Book to Remember™
Published by Flyleaf Publishing
Post Office Box 287, Lyme, NH 03768

For orders or information, contact us at **(800) 449-7006**.
Please visit our website at **www.flyleafpublishing.com**

First Edition
Library of Congress Catalog Card Number: 2002090760
Hard cover ISBN 1-929262-07-8
Soft cover ISBN 1-929262-08-6

For Terry

LAS

For Kari and Ajani

KW

A lot happens in the park at lunchtime...

Kids run and kick and toss balls.
They play hopscotch and tag.

Moms and dads and kids picnic on blankets
under the branches of trees.

Each day Mr. Sanchez has lunch in the park.
He sits on a bench under the branch of a big elm tree.

He hitches his dog Patch to the leg of the bench
and rests his lunch bag on his lap.

The kids in the park think Mr. Sanchez is a grump because he sits by himself each day.

Mr. Sanchez just sits on the bench and tosses bits of
his sandwich to the finches that nest in the big elm tree.

Each day the kids play kick ball; but not Roberto.

Roberto never gets picked for kick ball.

He cannot kick or pitch or catch well.

When the ball is kicked out the kids tell Roberto, "Go get it," and Roberto has to fetch it.

One day the ball is kicked out.
It lands on the patch of grass in front of Mr. Sanchez.

The kids yell, "Go get the ball from The Grump, Roberto!"

Roberto flinches as he asks Mr. Sanchez
for the ball back.

Mr. Sanchez just sits still.

At last, Mr. Sanchez picks up the ball
and tosses it back to the kids. What a toss!

The kids stop and watch the ball as it lands
smack-dab in front of the pitcher.

"You do not have to fetch for the rest of the kids,"
Mr. Sanchez tells Roberto.

"But I cannot toss or pitch or kick. I never get picked,"
Roberto frets.

"I can help," Mr. Sanchez tells him.

"Ask your parents if it is O.K. for me to help you.
If it is, bring a ball and we can toss and catch and kick."

The next day Roberto visits Mr. Sanchez at his bench.
Roberto has a red ball in his hands.

They kick and toss and catch. Mr. Sanchez is fantastic, but Roberto misses the ball a lot. "Watch the ball," Mr. Sanchez tells him.

When Mr. Sanchez has to rest, they sit on the bench and toss bits of their lunches to the finches.

Mr. Sanchez tells Roberto about his past as a ball player.

Mr. Sanchez and Roberto play each day until Roberto can toss and catch and kick very well.

One day on the bench, Mr. Sanchez tells Roberto, "I think you will get picked for kick ball if you ask to play."

"I think I will too," Roberto grins.

Roberto asks to play.

He is picked last, but he is not sad.
He understands that this is his chance...

The kids gasp when Roberto has a fantastic catch.

Mr. Sanchez claps and the kids yell
when Roberto has the best kick.

Roberto is the kick ball champ!

The next kick ball match Roberto is picked
to be the pitcher.

"No thank you," Roberto tells the kids.
"I am having lunch with Mr. Sanchez.
I will pitch for you next time."

Mr. Sanchez and The Kick Ball Champ is decodable with the 26 phonetic alphabet sounds plus the "ch" and "tch" phonograms, and the ability to blend those sounds together.

Puzzle Words are words used in the story that are either irregular or may have sound/spelling correspondences that the reader may not be familiar with.

The **Puzzle Word Review List** contains Puzzle Words that have been introduced in in previous books in the *Books to Remember* Series.

Please Note: If all of the words on this page are pre-taught and the reader knows the 26 phonetic alphabet sounds, plus the phonograms listed above, and has the ability to blend those sounds together, this book is 100% phonetically decodable.

Puzzle Words:	Puzzle Word Review List:		"ch/tch" words:
because	a	thank	bench
ball	as	that	branch
chance	be	the	branches
day	by	their	catch
each	do	they	champ
lunchtime	for	think	chance
Mr.	from	this	chat
O.K.	front	time	each
park	go	to	fetch
play	has	too	finches
player	have	tree	flinches
Roberto	having	trees	hitches
very	he	visits	hopscotch
	I	was	lunch
	is	we	lunches
	me	what	lunchtime
	no	when	match
	of	with	Patch
	one	you	pitch
	or	your	pitcher
	out		Sanchez
			sandwich
			watch

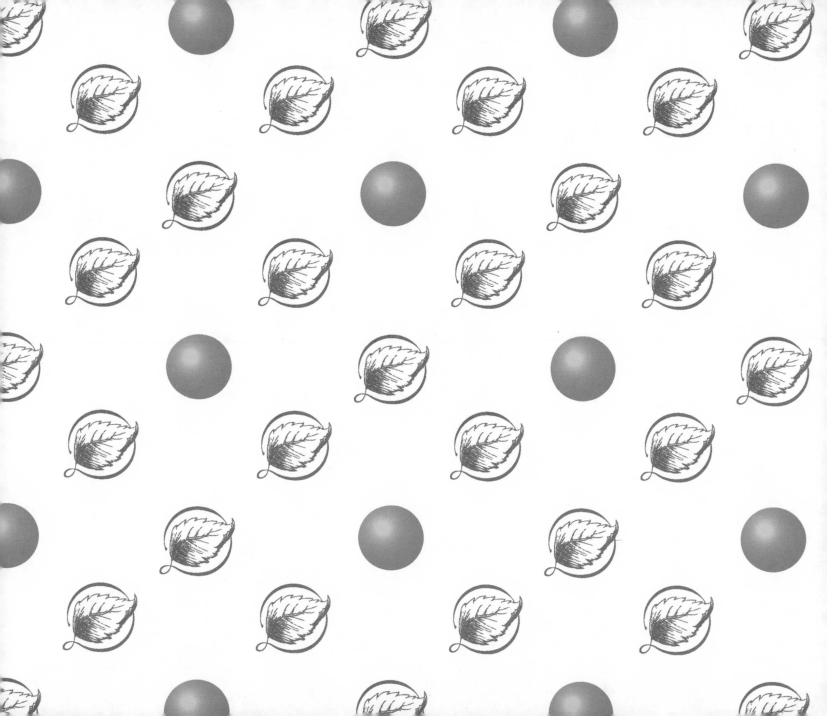

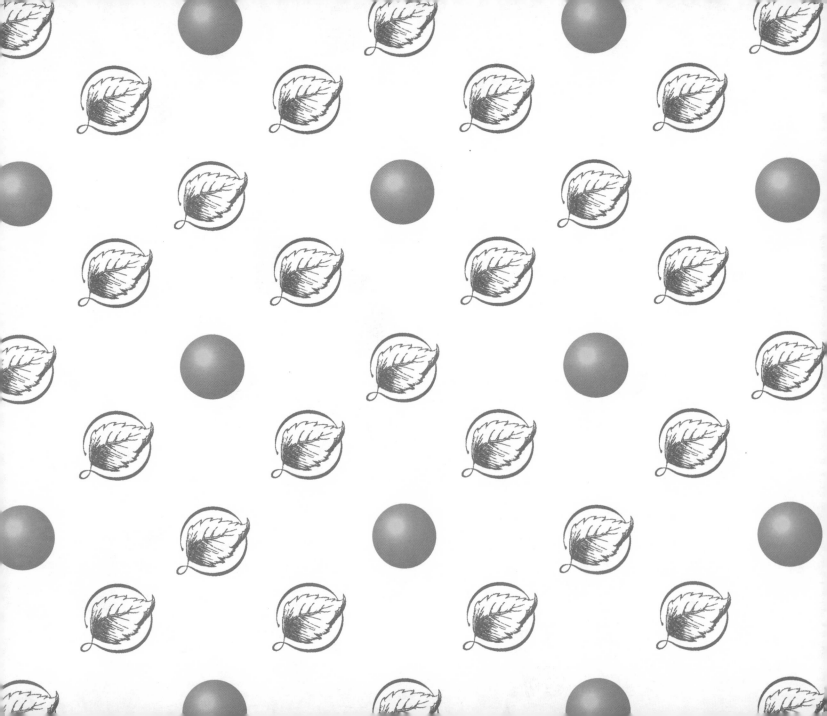